Dakota

Written by:Lili Paradis

Illustrated by: Katherine Paradis

www.liliwrites.com

ISBN Paperback: 979-8-88759-727-0
ISBN eBook: 979-8-88759-728-7
ISBN Hardcover: 979-8-88759-759-1

Dakota
LILI PARADIS

For my daughter Nina, with love

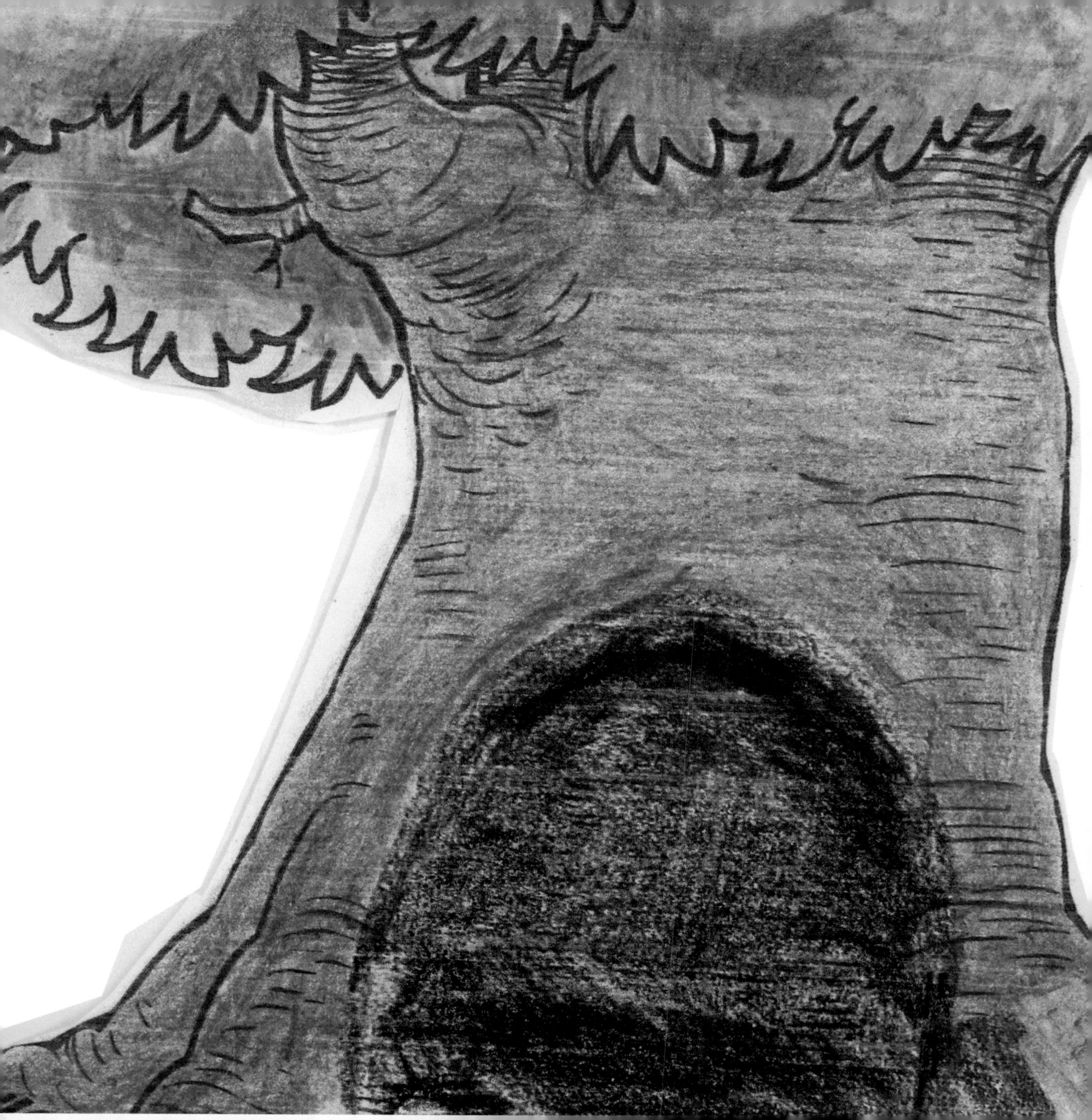

Dakota was born on a stormy day in a small hollow in the forest. His mother, Gaia, told him stories about it all the time, especially now that they had left the hollow and were headed towards the north, where something called the **Northern Lights** lay.

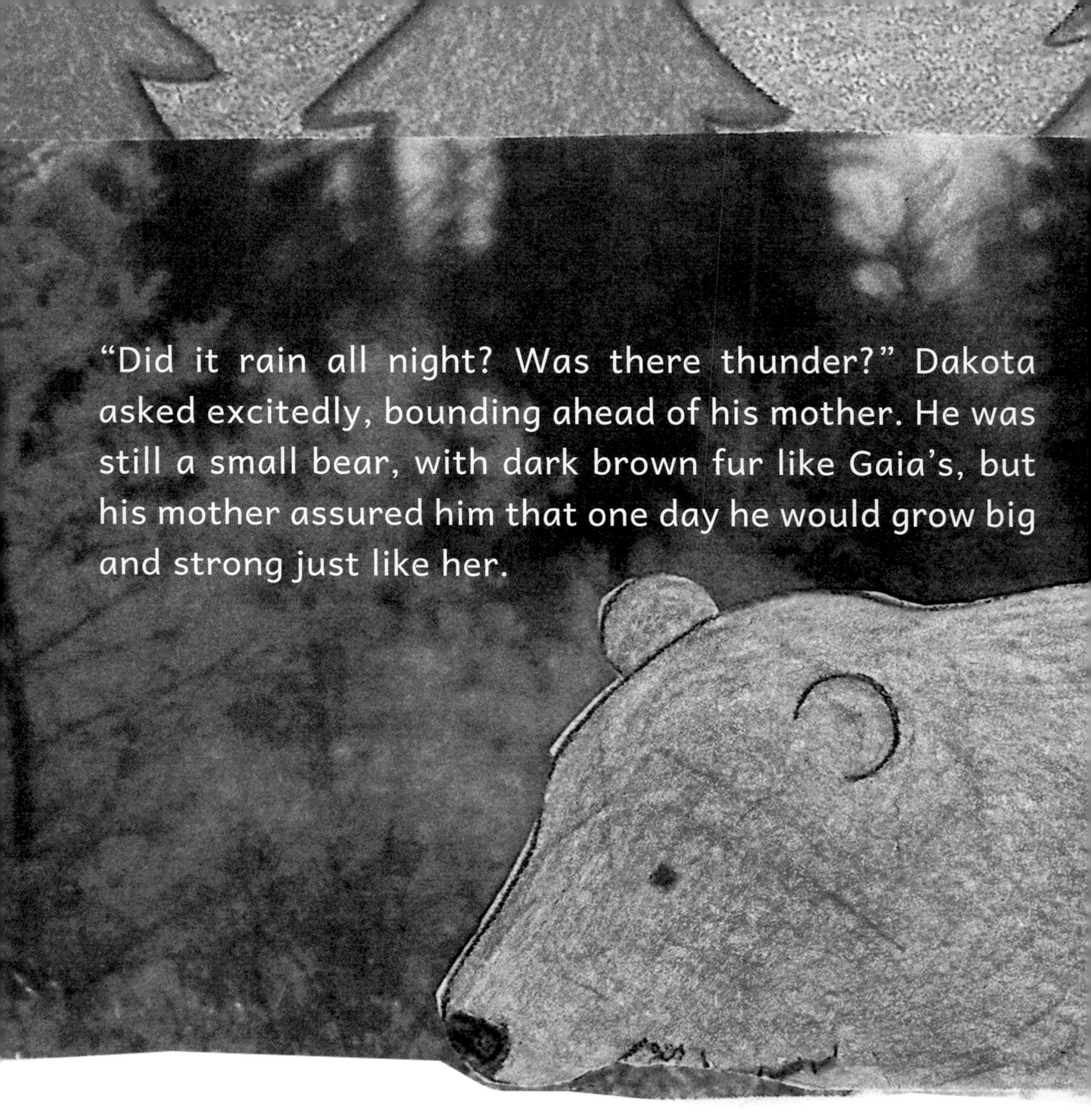

"Did it rain all night? Was there thunder?" Dakota asked excitedly, bounding ahead of his mother. He was still a small bear, with dark brown fur like Gaia's, but his mother assured him that one day he would grow big and strong just like her.

"It did, little bear. And there was."
Gaia plodded alongside her son.
"How long have we been walking, Mama?
It feels like it's been *ages!*" The journey seemed endless
to Dakota, but Gaia promised it wasn't.

“It’s only been three days, dear,” she said, laughing and smiling at her son. Dakota grew even more excited when the mountains began to appear, stretching towards the horizon like a line of mismatched, jagged teeth.

“We follow the mountains,” Gaia told him, chuckling under her breath as he made his way through the flowers. “But slow down, or you’ll tire yourself out!”

That night, the two lay curled up together beside the stream. Dakota asked his mother, “What are we doing tomorrow, Mama?”
“Well,” said Gaia, “I’m going to teach you how to catch salmon.” “But why, Mama?” Dakota asked. “You always catch the fish for us.”
“That’s true, little bear,” Gaia responded gently. “But one day, you’ll go on this journey alone. And when you do, you’ll need to know how to hunt for yourself.”

The next day, Gaia showed Dakota how to catch salmon. They stood at the top of the waterfall, watching in amazement as the fish jumped clean over it and into the river above. “Wow!” Dakota exclaimed.
“Interesting, isn’t it?” Gaia said. “The salmon always swim upstream.” Then, reaching her bushy head into the river, she effortlessly plucked a fat pink fish out of the water. “Like this, little bear.”
Dakota couldn’t imagine doing it as easily as his mother did. “I don’t think I can,” he said, shrinking away from the water.

“Of course, you can.” Gaia pushed her son gently forward with her nose. Dakota huffed and dunked his head into the water, shocking cold rushing around him, but came back up moments later empty-mouthed.
“Don’t worry, little bear,” his mother said. “Just keep practicing. You’ll be a pro before you know it.”

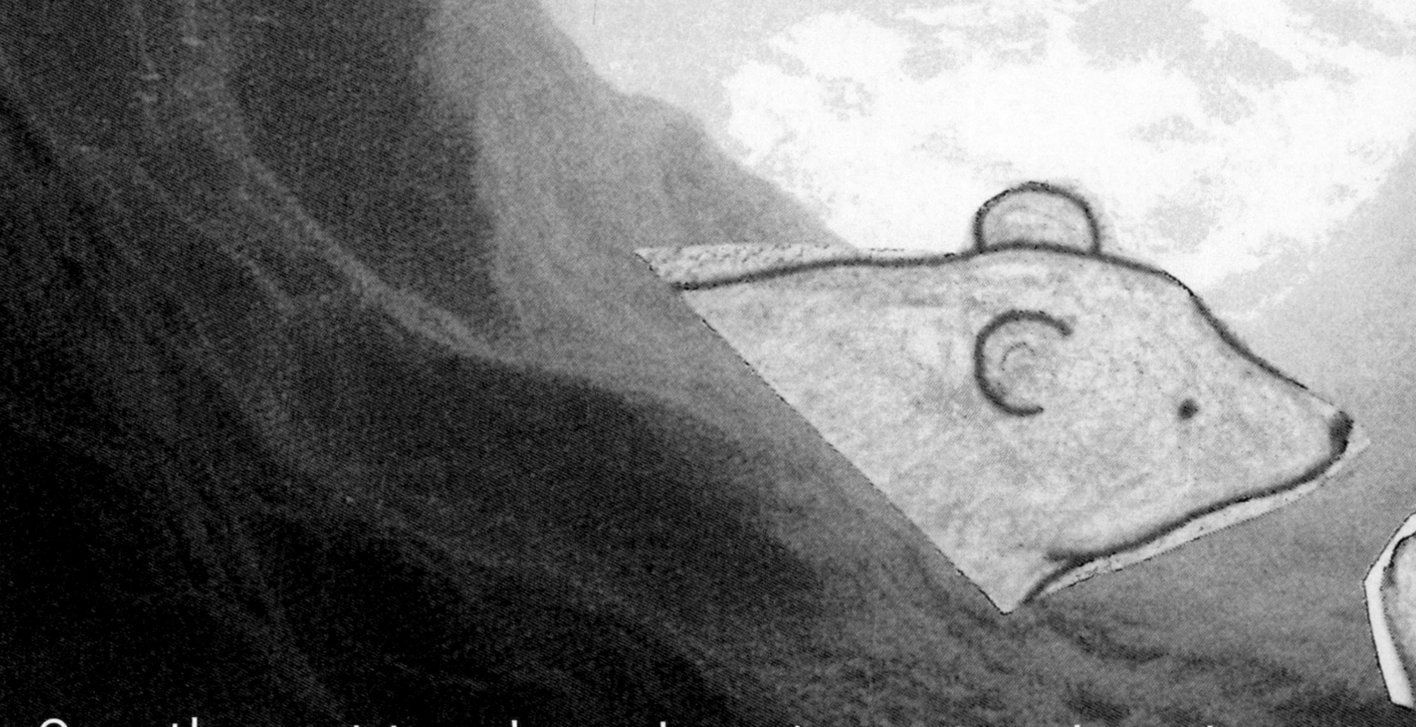

Over the next two days, the pair continued north, and the colder it became. Soon, grass and trees gave way to freezing cold snow and ice, glittering in the sunlight.
"It's cold, Mama," Dakota said, shivering.
"I know," Gaia said, "that's why we need to build a nice, snowy fort to rest in. If we stay inside, it will keep us warm."

When the night began to fall, they stopped at the bottom of a cliff. Gaia began to pack snow together until she had created a large fort.
"How did you do that, Mama?" Dakota asked in wonder as the two began to squeeze through the tiny door Gaia had made. "It just takes practice," she said. "Tomorrow, I'll show you how."

The next day, as the sun began to set, casting streaks of red across the ice, Gaia said, “Guess what, Dakota? We’re almost there.”

Dakota jumped with excitement and started to run. The ice, however, was much more slippery than he imagined, and he immediately fell, his paws scrambling as he tried to catch himself.

Gaia let out a hardy laugh from behind him. “Careful, little bear,” she chided gently. “You have to walk very slowly on the ice. Or, you can do this.” Carefully, Gaia lowered herself and began to belly-slide across the wide expanse of ground.

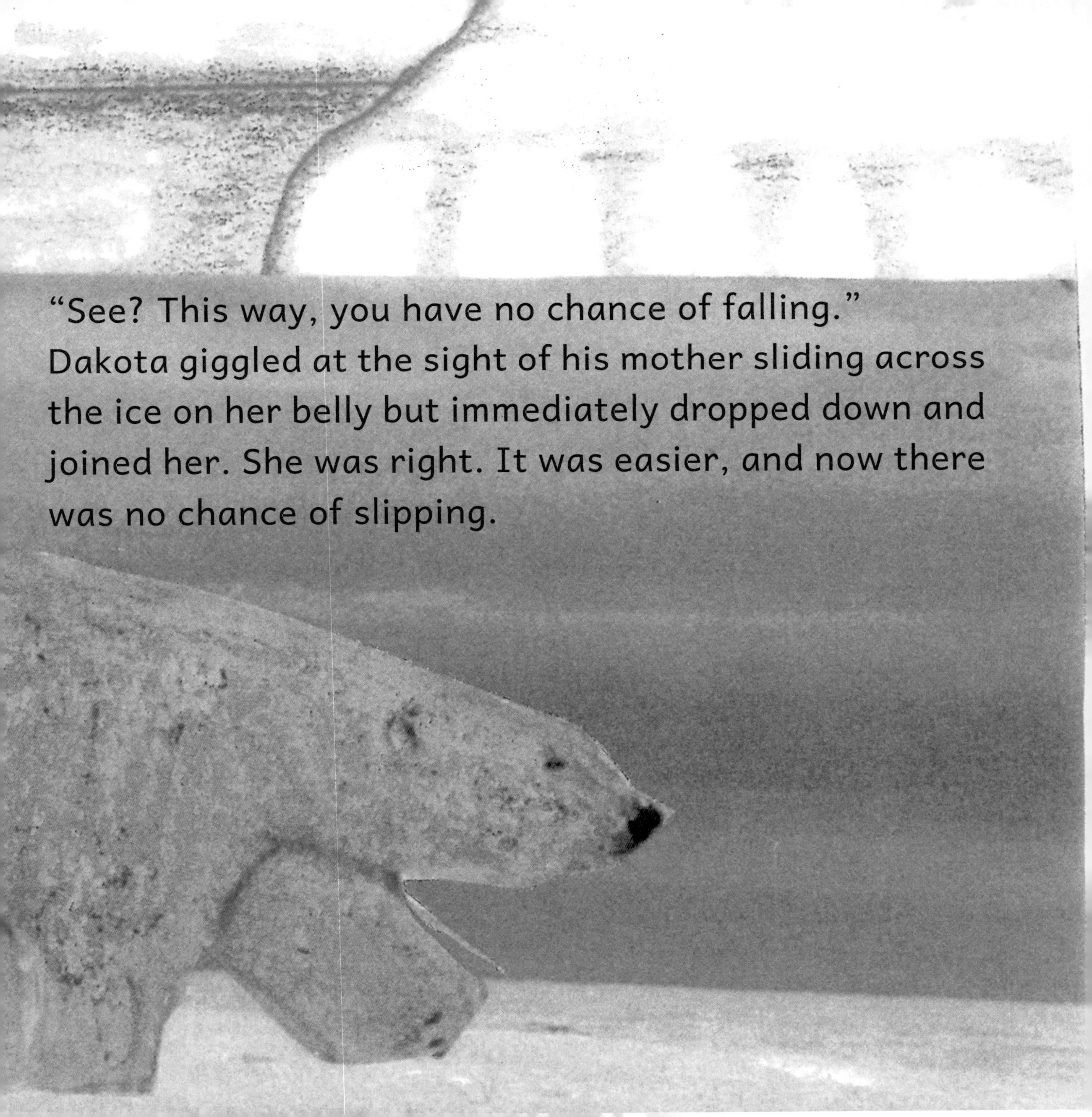

"See? This way, you have no chance of falling."
Dakota giggled at the sight of his mother sliding across the ice on her belly but immediately dropped down and joined her. She was right. It was easier, and now there was no chance of slipping.

Finally, the two bears arrived at the edge of the sea. The sky was turning a strange color of green, and as Dakota watched in awe, a ribbon of white, yellow, and pink began to snake through the sky, fluttering and changing colors as it seemingly rippled in the breeze.

"Wow," Dakota breathed, amazed at what he was seeing.

"Beautiful, isn't it?" Gaia said, reaching down to nuzzle her baby on the head.

"Yes," Dakota whispered and leaned into the comfort of his mother.

Every year, Dakota and his mother would make the journey from their home in the forest all the way to the land of the ice, where the Northern Lights lay. It was Dakota's favorite time of the year.
Every time they went, Gaia would help her son practice how to fish, build caves, and slide across the ice. Eventually, after many years, Dakota was so skilled that he didn't even need her help.

When the leaves began to turn each year, the emerald green giving way to ruby reds and buttery yellows, Dakota awoke on that special day with excitement, excited for their journey. He turned to his mother, nudging her with his nose. He was much bigger than Gaia now, and his fur had turned darker than ever. She had always told him this day would come, but he didn't realize it would happen so fast.

“Mama,” Dakota said.
“It’s time to start our journey!
We have to see the **Northern Lights!**”

This year, something was different. “Actually, my big bear,” his mother said sleepily, lifting her head up to smile at him, “today is the day you start your journey.”

“You’re not coming with me? But you always come with me!” Dakota protested, confused.

“Not this time,” Gaia said. “I’ve gotten too old to make the trip to the land of the ice now. But that’s okay. I’ve seen it many times in my life. And now, I’ve taught you how to do it alone.”

“Are you sure, Mama?” Dakota asked. He was a little scared; how was he supposed to do it without her?
“Positive,” Gaia said. “You are a grown bear now.”

So, sighing and burying his massive head into his mother’s fur one more time for luck, Dakota turned and set off by himself.

He walked slowly to conserve energy, caught plenty of fish, and built a fort the way Gaia had shown him. He thought of his mother as he stepped lightly over the pine needles blanketing the forest floor.

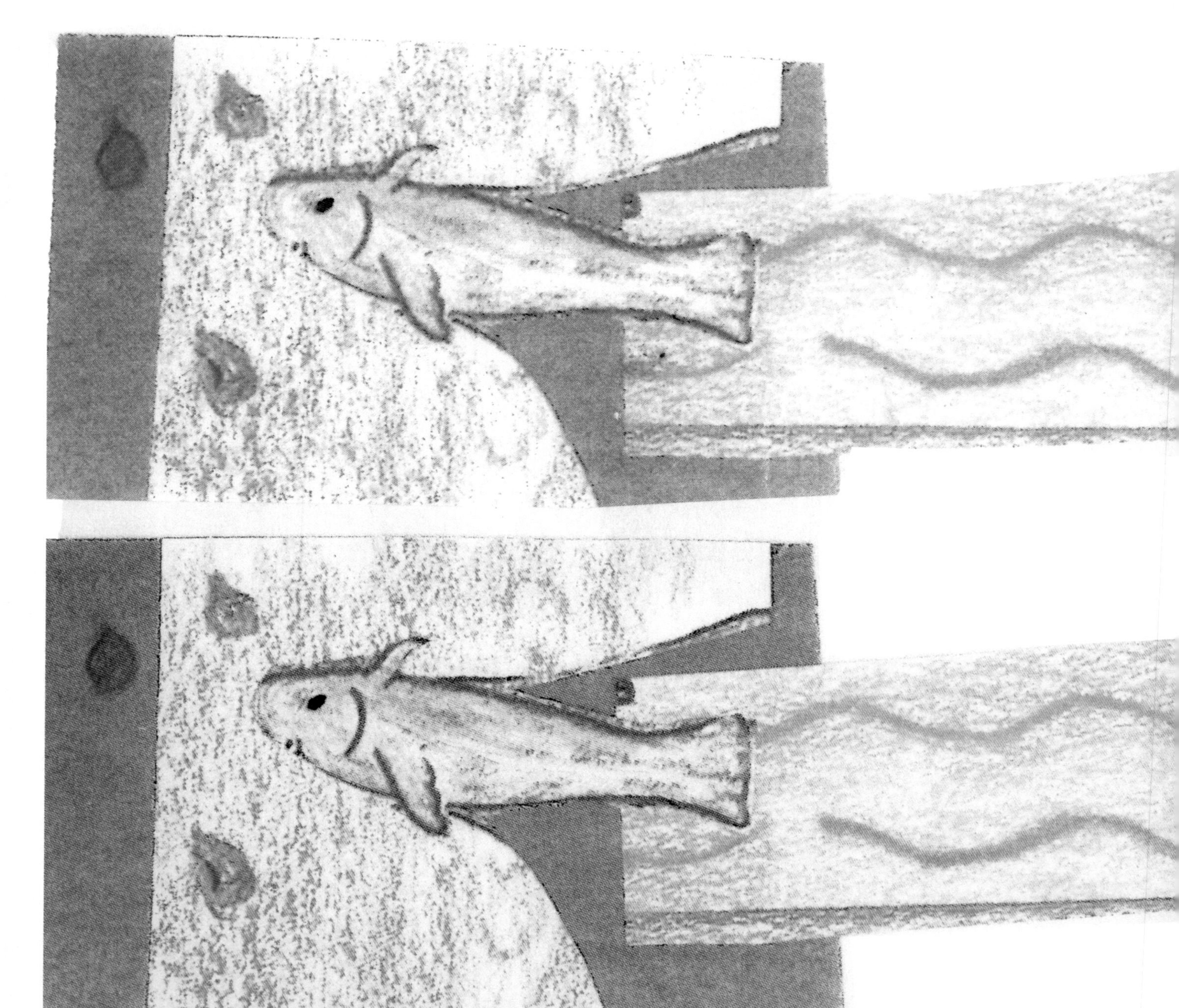

He thought of her again while he was watching the salmon dance towards him in an arc, rainbow drops spraying across the sky.

As night fell, the sky turning an incredibly dark color of blue, Dakota built his fort, imagining Gaia's paws as he packed the snow together.

And finally, when he got to the ice, he lowered himself onto his belly and slid across with ease, giggling under his breath as he thought just how silly he must look.

Finally, Dakota got to the Northern Lights. He watched in awe as they danced across the sky, looking just as beautiful as the first time he'd seen them. He swore he could almost feel his mother's shoulder pressed into his cheek, holding him up after the long journey.

He looked into the sky, alight with color. It had never stopped amazing him. “Wow,” he whispered, taking it all in. “Thanks, Mama.”

Acknowledgments

I wouldn't have been able to do this without the constant support of my family. To my dad, thank you for always sharing your love of writing with me. To Devin, thank you for always being there for me while I've embarked on my new career. And a special thank you to my mother, for agreeing to take on this passion project with me. Being able to collaborate on this with you has been so special.

About the Author

Although she grew up in the American south, Lili is originally from Ontario, so her love of grizzly bears, snow, and all things Great White North runs deep. She is a freelance writer, novelist, and currently works in immigration law specializing in human rights violations. Lili lives in North Carolina with her partner, daughter, and a menagerie of animals. You can visit her online at www.liliwrites.com

All proceeds from the sale of this book will benefit the Ajo Samaritans and Team Brownsville, nonprofit organizations providing humanitarian relief to asylum seekers and the migrant community as a whole.

Made in the USA
Columbia, SC
11 November 2023